FRANNIE'S FRUITS

by Leslie Kimmelman   pictures by Petra Mathers

Harper & Row, Publishers

Frannie's Fruits
Text copyright © 1989 by Leslie A. Kimmelman
Illustrations copyright © 1989 by Petra Mathers

Library of Congress Cataloging-in-Publication Data

Kimmelman, Leslie.
    Frannie's fruits / by Leslie Kimmelman ; pictures by Petra Mathers.
        p.   cm.
    Summary: A little girl and her family operate a fruit and
vegetable stand near the beach with the help of their dog Frannie.
    ISBN 0-06-023143-2 : $ ISBN 0-06-023164-5 (lib. bdg.) : $
    [1. Business enterprises—Fiction.   2. Stores, Retail—Fiction.
3. Beaches—Fiction.   4. Dogs—Fiction.]   I. Mathers, Petra, ill.
II. Title.
PZ7.K56493Fr 1989   88-17637
[E]—dc 19   CIP
                                               AC

Printed in the U.S.A. All rights reserved.
1 2 3 4 5 6 7 8 9 10
First Edition

My family has a fruit stand on Highway 57. It is called Frannie's Fruits. Frannie is our dog.

Frannie's Fruits is open from the end of May until the beginning of September—when the summer people are here. We sell fresh fruits and vegetables and even pick-your-own flowers.

On Saturdays we open early. Everyone helps. My brother, John, puts all the vegetables out—first the lettuce and cabbage, then the zucchini, then the corn and tomatoes and green beans and all the rest. He even polishes the green peppers.

My older sister, Katie, arranges the fruit. The colors look like the crayons in my crayon box. There are red apples, purple plums, green grapes, blueberries and strawberries and raspberries, oranges and lemons and limes, watermelons and honeydew melons and cantaloupes.

Mom makes sure the flowers are watered and fresh looking. Dad sweeps the floor and dusts the shelves. I walk around for a last-minute check. I make sure all the signs are right.

Carrots, 25¢ a pound

a dozen eggs for 79¢

raspberries, $1.05 a basket

"Frannie, get your nose out of that corn!" I say. I make a sign for my Mr. Potato Head doll—

POTATOES FOR POTATO HEADS!

—and put him on the shelf.

"ROWF, ROWF, ROWF," barks Frannie happily. She's telling everyone we're open for business.

Our first customer is Mr. Tupper. He comes every single morning and buys the same thing each time.

"Two tomatoes, Tom," he says to my father. "They're terribly tasty." And, after he pays for them, "Toodle-oo!"

Next to come by is Mrs. Crinch. Her order is the same each time too—a dozen lemons. "I bet she eats lemons all day long," Katie whispers to me. "Her mouth is stuck in a pucker, the old sourpuss."

I giggle.

Dad is helping another customer choose some sweet corn when Joanna comes in. Joanna is my best friend. Her mother has sent her for some strawberries. With her dark sunburn and the freckles all over her face, Joanna looks like a strawberry herself. She gets some peaches, too, and I weigh them on our scale.

"I'll see you later," I tell her, waving good-bye.

A lady artist stops by for some flowers to paint. I wish *I* could paint—I would paint her and the flowers together.

It's getting to be lunchtime, and Dad makes a big tossed salad for everyone. Katie picks out the mushrooms and cauliflower. She doesn't like the way they taste. I bite into a juicy tomato, and it squirts all over my chin.

A lady with a toothy smile sees the bottle of mustard vinegar dressing and asks if we sell it. "No," replies Katie, "it's my dad's special recipe."

"Too bad," she says. But she buys some vegetables anyway.

After lunch, I go for a run with Frannie to stretch my legs. When I return, Mom is talking to Mr. Vanderman, who's stopped by to pick up some blackberries for his wife.

"Addie makes the best blackberry cobbler you've ever tasted," he brags. "Come by later for a taste."

"Are you sure it's all right?" asks Mom.

"She'd love seeing you folks," Mr. Vanderman answers her.
"Bring the kids and we'll make it a party." And he waves good-bye.
I love going to the Vandermans' house. For one thing, their
backyard has the best climbing tree in town.

Some more customers come in, and I'm kept busy weighing and putting things in bags. John puts more corn in the bins and restocks the shelves.

A lady with a gigantic, crazy-looking hat asks, "Do you have any fresh pineapples?" John shows her where the pineapples are, and the lady lifts a couple of them to her nose and sniffs. "I'll take this one," she says.

A bunch of boys come in straight off the beach, still in their bathing suits. They act like they've had too much sun. They pick out some bananas and coconuts, and pretend to be monkeys. Frannie gets all excited, jumping up and down and barking, and we have to quiet her down after the boys leave.

A skinny man buys a pound of asparagus, and a woman with six small children leaves with six bags overflowing. A pregnant lady carries a dozen kumquats to her car, laughing. "I can't seem to stop eating these things," she says.

It is getting late now, and the stand is crowded with people on their way home from the beach. Dad keeps sweeping sand off the floor. I hold the dustpan. Then I see Joanna up near the cash register and wave to her. As soon as I finish helping Dad, Joanna and I set up our lemonade table, just like we do every afternoon. Everyone is thirsty from the hot sun, and we sell out after an hour.

A young couple comes in, and Mom points them to the flower field. When they return, the boy is carrying the biggest bouquet of flowers I've ever seen.

"These flowers are to remind you of today," I hear him saying. "And they're only half as pretty as you are."

The girl kisses him on the cheek.

"Isn't that romantic?" sighs Katie as she watches them leave.

But Joanna and I just giggle.

It's almost closing time. Joanna has left. Mom is counting the money in the register. Dad serves a last-minute customer who is buying an enormous watermelon. The melon is so huge, Dad has to help him carry it to his car. John loads some fruits and vegetables into the back of our pickup truck. The rest will stay in the stand until we open again tomorrow. Katie gathers some flowers to take to Mrs. Vanderman tonight, and I run after Frannie.

"Okay, everyone," announces Dad. "Time to go home."

"ROWF, ROWF," barks Frannie. We're closed for the night, she's saying. She jumps into the back of the truck with Katie and me.

I close my eyes, but still I can see rows and rows of brightly colored vegetables and fruits. Tomorrow I'm spending the day on the beach. "You can come too," I tell Frannie. "You can chase sea gulls or hunt for hermit crabs while Joanna and I build sand castles and jump waves."

I lean back against a sack of corn and watch the sun set over the bay. Frannie and I snuggle together as the truck rounds a bend. We're glad the summer's just beginning.